ROUND ABOUT SIX

compiled by Margaret G. Rawlins with illustrations by Denis Wrigley

ROUND ABOUT SIX

FREDERICK WARNE

Published by
FREDERICK WARNE (PUBLISHERS) LTD: *London*
FREDERICK WARNE & CO INC: *New York*

© *Frederick Warne & Co Ltd*
London, England, 1973

Reprinted 1975 and 1981

Margaret Rawlins has studied the interests of young
children for many years and here offers a particularly
fresh collection of poems for the 'round about sixes'.
It is part of a very successful series and is
intended in its age appeal to complement *Fives, Sixes
and Sevens*, which has enjoyed wide popularity.

Many of the poems are by well-known poets such as
Roy Fuller, Spike Milligan, Ted Hughes and
Elizabeth Jennings. Among American poets represented
are Ogden Nash and Lois Lenski. Several of the poems
have been written by children.

Again, Denis Wrigley's amusing illustrations enhance
the book and bring gaiety to this varied collection.

Library of Congress Catalog Card No 73-80254

ISBN 0 7232 1728 9
Printed in Great Britain by
BAS Printers Limited, Over Wallop, Hampshire
D 6453.1280

Contents

Seven and a Half

Acknowledgements

The compiler and publishers wish to thank the following for their kind permission to reproduce poems:

Five and a Half

Shel Silverstein for "Oh, Who Will Wash the Tiger's Ears?"; Clive Sansom for "The Rabbit and the Fox" and "Mice and Cat" from *The Golden Unicorn* published by Methuen & Co. Ltd; Dennis Dobson for "I'm Not Frightened of Pussy Cats" from *Silly Verse for Kids* by Spike Milligan; Ian Serraillier for "The Tickle Rhyme" and "The Mouse in the Wainscot"; Evans Brothers Ltd for "The Swing" by Mary I. Osborn from *A Book of a Thousand Poems*; The World Publishing Company for "There Was a Young Lady of Spain" and "There Was a Small Maiden Named Maggie" from *Limerick Giggles, Joke Giggles* published by The Bodley Head Ltd; A. & C. Black Ltd for "The Engine Driver" from *Speech Rhymes* by Clive Sansom; the Estate of the late Miss Eleanor Farjeon for "Mrs. Peck-Pigeon" from *Nursery Rhymes of London Town*; Gerald Duckworth & Co. Ltd for "The Elephant" from *The Bad Child's Book of Beasts* by Hilaire Belloc; André Deutsch Ltd for "Epitaph" and "Bringing Up Babies" from *Seen Grandpa Lately?* by Roy Fuller; Macmillan London and Basingstoke for "The Hamster" by Elizabeth Jennings from *The Secret Brother and Other Poems*.

"My Puppy" is from *Up the Windy Hill* by Aileen Fisher. Reprinted by permission of Scott, Foresman and Company. "The Elephant" is also from *Cautionary Verses*, by Hilaire Belloc. Published 1941 by Alfred A. Knopf, Inc. Reprinted by permission of the publisher.

Six and a Half

The Brockhampton Press Ltd for "Johnny's Pockets" by Alison Winn from *Helter Skelter*; Miss Caryl Brahms for "The King's High Drummer"; the Estate of the late Miss Eleanor Farjeon for "King's Cross" from *Nursery Rhymes of London Town*; Evans Brothers Ltd for "The Song of the Engine" by H. Worsley-Benison, "The Tadpole" by E. E. Gould and "High June" by Catherine A. Morin from *A Book of a Thousand Poems*; Dennis Dobson for "A Baby Sardine" from *A Book of Milliganimals* and "The Hippo-rhinostricow" from *Silly Verse for Kids* both by Spike Milligan; Oxford University Press for "The Black Pebble" from *The Blackbird in the Lilac* by James Reeves; Miss Kathy Henderson for "The Dragon with the Big Nose"; "Noise" from *Children as Poets* edited by D. Thompson, published by Chatto & Windus Ltd; the Literary Trustees of Walter de la Mare, and The Society of Authors as their representative for "A-Apple Pie" and "Quack"; André Deutsch Ltd for "Horrible Things" from *Seen Grandpa Lately?* by Roy Fuller; John Tompkins for "Snail"; Gerald Duckworth & Co. Ltd for "The Dodo" from *The Bad Child's Book of Beasts* by Hilaire Belloc; the Estate of the late Ogden Nash for "Winter Morning" from *Parents Keep Out*.

"Folks" by Ted Hughes is reprinted by permission of Faber and Faber Ltd from *Meet My Folks!* "White Fields" is from *Collected Poems* by James Stephens, by permission of Mrs. Iris Wise, Macmillan

Five and a Half

Contents

My Puppy

It's funny
my puppy
knows just how I feel.

When I'm happy
he's yappy
and squirms like an eel.

When I'm grumpy
he's slumpy
and stays at my heel.

It's funny
my puppy
knows such a great deal.

AILEEN FISHER

How Many Cherries?

How many cherries
Have you got?
Eat up your cherries
On the spot,
Count your cherry stones,
Learn your lot,
Are you lucky
Or are you not?

Tinker, tailor
Soldier, sailor
Richman, Poorman
Beggarman—Thief.

UNKNOWN

Oh, Who Will Wash the Tiger's Ears?

Oh, who will wash the tiger's ears?
And who will comb his tail?
And who will brush his sharp white teeth?
And who will file his nails?

Oh, Bobby may wash the tiger's ears
And Susy may file his nails
And Lucy may brush his long white teeth
And I'll go down for the mail.

SHEL SILVERSTEIN

5

The Rabbit and the Fox

A rabbit came hopping, hopping,
Hopping along in the park.
"I've just been shopping, shopping,
I must be home before dark."

A fox came stalking, stalking,
Stalking from under a tree.
"Where are you walking, walking?
Why don't you walk with me?"

The rabbit went hopping, hopping,
Hopping away from the tree.
"I've just been shopping, shopping,
I must be home for my tea."

"Come with me, bunny, bunny—
Bunny, you come with me;
I'll give you some honey, honey,
I'll give you some honey for tea."

"I can't be stopping, stopping,
I'm far too busy today"—
And the rabbit went hopping, hopping,
Hopping away and away.

CLIVE SANSOM

Elephant Rhymes

Way down South where bananas grow,
A grasshopper stepped on an elephant's toe.
The elephant said, with tears in his eyes,
"Pick on somebody your own size."

The elephant carries a great big trunk;
He never packs it with clothes;
It has no lock and it has no key,
But he takes it wherever he goes.

UNKNOWN

I'm Not Frightened of Pussy Cats

I'm not frightened of Pussy Cats,
They only eat up mice and rats,
But a hippopotamus
Could eat the Lotofus.

SPIKE MILLIGAN

The Tickle Rhyme

"Who's that tickling my back?" said the wall.
"Me," said a small
Caterpillar. "I'm learning
To crawl."

IAN SERRAILLIER

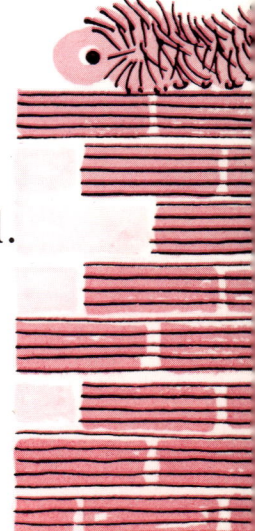

Riddles

What thing am I?

Riddle me! riddle me! What is that
Over your head and under your hat?
Answer: HAIR

A milk-white bird
Floats down through the air
And never a tree
But he lights there.
Answer: SNOW

It has a head like a cat, feet like a cat,
A tail like a cat, but it isn't a cat.
Answer: A KITTEN

UNKNOWN

10

The Swing

Now so high,
Now so low,
Up in the air,
Then down I go.
Up to the sky,
Down to the grass,
I watch birds fly,
I see worms pass.

With feet in front
And hair behind,
I race the birds,
I race the wind,
Over the world,
Under the tree,
Nobody knows
What things I see.
Wonderful lanes
Where children play
From early morn
All thro' the day.

MARY I. OSBORN

The Mulberry Bush

Here we go round the mulberry bush,
The mulberry bush, the mulberry bush,
Here we go round the mulberry bush
On a cold and frosty morning.

This is the way we wash our hands,
Wash our hands, wash our hands,
This is the way we wash our hands,
On a cold and frosty morning.

This is the way we clean our teeth,
Clean our teeth, clean our teeth,
This is the way we clean our teeth,
On a cold and frosty morning.

This is the way we brush our hair,
Brush our hair, brush our hair,
This is the way we brush our hair,
On a cold and frosty morning.

This is the way we run to school,
Run to school, run to school,
This is the way we run to school,
On a cold and frosty morning.

UNKNOWN

Song Without End

The bear went over the mountain,
The bear went over the mountain,
The bear went over the mountain,
And what do you think he saw?

He saw another mountain,
He saw another mountain,
He saw another mountain,
And what do you think he did?

He climbed that other mountain,
He climbed that other mountain,
He climbed that other mountain,
And what do you think he saw?

He saw another mountain,
He saw . . . .

UNKNOWN

Two Limericks

There was a small maiden named Maggie,
Whose dog was enormous and shaggy;
    The front end of him
    Looked vicious and grim—
But the tail end was friendly and waggy.

There was a young lady of Spain,
Who couldn't go out in the rain,
    'Cause she'd lent her umbrella
    To Queen Isabella
Who never returned it again.

WILLIAM COLE

Whisky Frisky

Whisky Frisky,
Hipperty hop,
Up he goes
To the tree top!

Whirly, twirly,
Round and round,
Down he scampers
To the ground.

Furly, curly,
What a tail,
Tall as a feather,
Broad as a sail.

Where's his supper?
In the shell.
Snappy, cracky,
Out it fell.

UNKNOWN

16

The Little Girl

There was a little girl, and she had a little curl
Right in the middle of her forehead;
When she was good she was very, very good,
But when she was bad she was horrid.

One day she went upstairs, while her parents,
    unawares,
In the kitchen were occupied with meals;
And she stood upon her head, on her little truckle-
    bed,
And then began hurraying with her heels.

Her mother heard the noise and thought it was the
    boys,
A-kicking up a rumpus in the attic;
But when she climbed the stair, and saw Jemima
    there,
She took her and did whip her most emphatic.

UNKNOWN

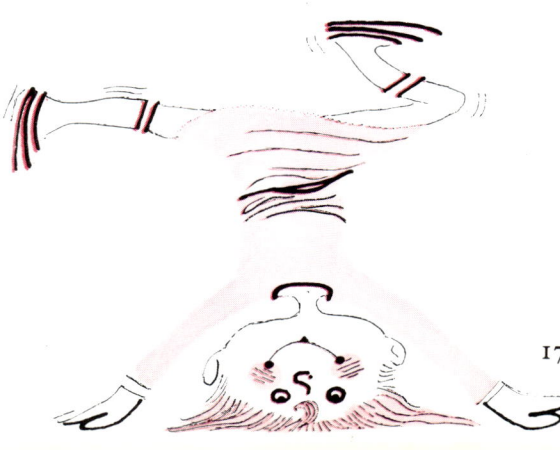

The Mouse in the Wainscot

Hush, Suzanne!
Don't lift your cup.
That breath you heard
Is a mouse getting up.

As the mist that streams
From your milk as you sup,
So soft is the sound
Of a mouse getting up.

There! did you hear
His feet pitter-patter,
Lighter than tipping
Of beads in a platter,

And then like a shower
On the window pane
The little feet scampering
Back again?

O falling of feather!
O drift of a leaf!
The mouse in the wainscot
Is dropping asleep.

IAN SERRAILLIER

The Engine Driver

The train goes running along the line,
Jicketty-can, jicketty-can.
I wish it were mine, I wish it were mine,
Jicketty-can, jicketty-can.
The engine driver stands in front,
He makes it run, he makes it shunt;
Out of the town,
Out of the town,
Over the hill,
Over the down,
Under the bridges,
Across the lea,
Over the ridge
And down to the sea,
With a jicketty-can, jicketty-can,
Jicketty-jicketty-jicketty-can
Jicketty-can, jicketty-can.

CLIVE SANSOM

Who's In?

"The door is shut fast
    And everyone's out."
But people don't know
    What they're talking about!
Say the fly on the wall,
And the flame on the coals,
And the dog on his rug,
And the mice in their holes,
And the kitten curled up,
And the spiders that spin—
"What, everyone's out?
    Why, everyone's in!"

ELIZABETH FLEMING

Algy No More

Algy met a bear,
The bear met Algy.
The bear grew bulgy—
The bulge was Algy.

UNKNOWN

Billy Boy

Billy Boy, Billy Boy, where are you riding to?
Riding old Dobbin to Banbury Fair.
Billy Boy, Billy Boy, will you be long away?
Just twice as long as it takes to get there.

Billy Boy, Billy Boy, what will you bring for me?
One golden fiddle to play a fine tune,
Two magic wishes and three fairy fishes,
And four rainbow ropes to climb up to the moon.

TRADITIONAL

Mrs. Peck-Pigeon

Mrs. Peck-Pigeon
Is pecking for bread,
Bob-bob-bob
Goes her little round head.
Tame as a pussy-cat
In the street,
Step-step-step
With her little red feet
And her little round head,
Mrs. Peck-Pigeon
Goes pecking for bread.

ELEANOR FARJEON

The Elephant

When people call this beast to mind,
They marvel more and more
At such a little tail behind
So LARGE a trunk before.

HILAIRE BELLOC

Mice and Cat

One mouse, two mice,
Three mice, four,
Stealing from their tunnel,
Creeping through the door.

Softly! Softly!
Don't make a sound—
Don't let your little feet
Patter on the ground.

There on the hearthrug,
Sleek and fat,
Soundly sleeping,
Lies old Tom Cat.

If he should hear you,
There'd be no more
Of one mouse, two mice,
Three mice, four.

So please be careful
How far you roam,
For if you should wake him . . .
He'd-chase-you-all-HOME!

CLIVE SANSOM

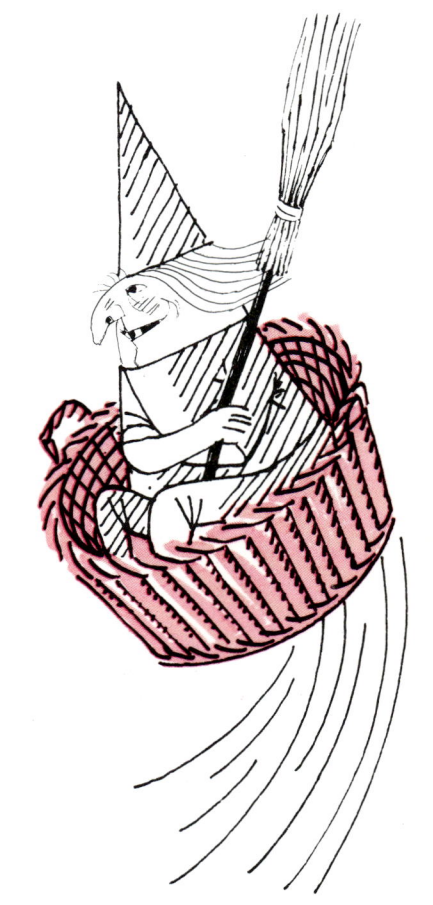

There Was an Old Woman

There was an old woman tossed up in a basket,
Seventeen times as high as the moon;
But where she was going, I couldn't but ask it,
For in her hand she carried a broom.

"Old woman, old woman, old woman," quoth I,
"O whither, O whither, O whither so high?"
"To sweep the cobwebs off the sky!"
"Shall I go with you?"
"Ay, by and by."

UNKNOWN

Little Johnny

Little Johnny fished all day,
Fishes would not come his way.
"Had enough of this," said he,
"I'll be going home to tea."

When the fishes saw him go,
Up they came all in a row;
Jumped about and laughed with glee,
Shouting, "Johnny's home to tea!"

UNKNOWN

A Little Talk

The big brown hen and Mrs. Duck
Went walking out together;
They talked about all sorts of things—
The farmyard, and the weather.
But all *I* heard was: "Cluck!
    Cluck! Cluck!"
And "Quack! Quack! Quack!"
    from Mrs. Duck.

UNKNOWN

Wishes

Said the first little chicken,
With a queer little squirm,
"I wish I could find
A fat little worm."

Said the next little chicken,
With a sharp little squeal,
"I wish I could find
Some nice yellow meal."

Said the third little chicken,
With a small sigh of grief,
"I wish I could find
A little green leaf."

"See here," said the mother,
From the green garden patch,
"If you want any breakfast,
Just come here and scratch."

UNKNOWN

Bird Song

Pigeon   Don't scold so, Susie
Don't scold so, Susie
Don't scold so, Susie
Don't.

Thrush   Pretty Dick, pretty Dick, pretty Dick.
Come here! Come here! Come here!
Dear! Dear! Dear!

Cuckoo   Cuckoo, Cuckoo,
Pray what do you do?
In April, I open my bill.
In May, I sing night and day.
In June, I change my tune.
In July, away I fly.
In August, away I must.

Cuckoo, Cuckoo,
Pray where do you go?
Up high, into the sky,
Far away over the sea,
To Spain, I fly again;
Day and night I take my flight.
Cuckoo.
Goodbye to you.

UNKNOWN

The Hamster

A hamster by name of Big Cheek
Stored up nuts that would last for a week.
Alas, he ignored
That their being so stored
Made him look the most terrible freak.

ELIZABETH JENNINGS

Two Little Kittens

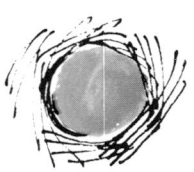

Two little kittens, one stormy night,
Began to quarrel, and then to fight.
One had a mouse and the other had none;
And that was the way the quarrel began.

"I'll have that mouse," said the bigger cat.
"You'll have that mouse? We'll see about that!"
"I will have that mouse!" said the older one.
"You shan't have that mouse!" said the little one.

I told you before 'twas a stormy night
When those two little kittens began to fight.
The old woman seized her sweeping broom,
And swept the two kittens right out of the room.

The ground was all covered with frost and snow,
And the two little kittens had nowhere to go.
So they laid them down on the mat at the door,
While the old woman finished sweeping the floor.

Then they both crept in as quiet as mice,
All wet with snow and as cold as ice.
For they found it much better that stormy night
To lie down and sleep, than to quarrel and fight.

JANE TAYLOR

If I Had a Donkey

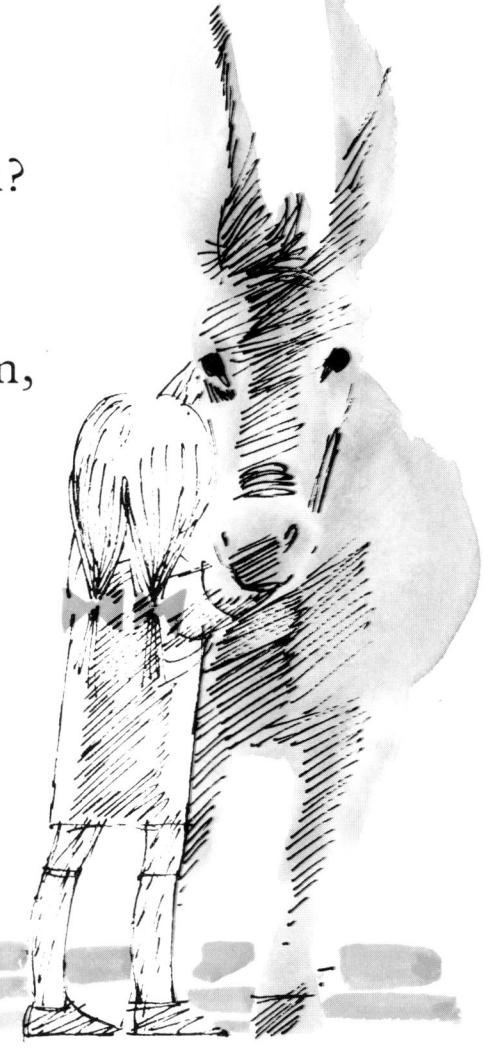

If I had a donkey
And he wouldn't go,
D'you think I'd wallop him?
No! No! No!
I'd put him in a stable
To keep him nice and warm,
The best little donkey
That ever was born.
Gee up, Neddy,
Gee up, Neddy,
The best little donkey
That ever was born.

NURSERY RHYME

Epitaph

Here lies a greedy girl, Jane Bevan,
Whose breakfasts hardly ever stopped.
One morning at half past eleven
She snapped and crackled and then popped.

UNKNOWN

Bringing Up Babies

If babies could only speak they'd tell mother or
        nurse
That slapping was pointless, and why:
For if you're not crying it prompts you to cry,
And if you are—then you cry worse.

ROY FULLER

Six and a Half

Contents

He leaves the Nest

He leaves the nest,
And flaps his wings,
And steps and struts,
And bit by bit,
He makes his way
To top of tree:
And,
His neck up,
His tail up,
His foot up,
The cock lifts
His voice up,
And,
Crows.

UNKNOWN

Folks

I've heard so much
    about other folks' folks,
How somebody's Uncle
    told such jokes
The cat split laughing
    and had to be stitched,
How somebody's Aunt
    got so bewitched
She fried the kettle
    and washed the water
And spanked a letter
    and posted her daughter.
Other folks' folk get so well known,
And nobody knows about my own.

TED HUGHES

The Crocodile

If you should meet a crocodile,
Don't take a stick and poke him;
Ignore the welcome in his smile,
Be careful not to stroke him.
For as he sleeps upon the Nile,
He thinner gets and thinner;
And whene'er you meet a crocodile
He's ready for his dinner.

UNKNOWN

Skipping Rhymes

I like coffee, I like tea,
I like the boys and the boys like me.
Tell your mother to hold her tongue,
For she did the same when she was young.
Tell your father to do the same,
For he was the one who changed her name.

"Hello, hello, hello, sir,
Meet me at the grocer."
"No, sir."
"Why, sir?"
"Because I have a cold, sir."
"Where did you get your cold, sir?"
"At the North Pole, sir."
"What were you doing there, sir?"
"Shooting polar bear, sir."
"Let me hear you sneeze, sir."
"Kachoo, kachoo, kachoo, sir."

UNKNOWN

Johnny's Pockets

Johnny collects
Conkers on strings,
Sycamore seeds
With aeroplane wings,
Green acorn cups,
Seaweed and shells,
Treasures from crackers
Like whistles and bells.

Johnny collects
Buttons and rings,
Bits of a watch,
Cog wheels and springs,
Half-eaten sweets,
Nuts, nails and screws.
That's why his pockets
Bulge out of his trews.

ALISON WINN

White Fields

In winter-time we go
Walking in the fields of snow;

Where there is no grass at all;
Where the top of every wall,

Every fence and every tree,
Is as white as white can be.

Pointing out the way we came—
Every one of them the same—

All across the fields there be
Prints in silver filigree:

And our mothers always know
By the footprints in the snow,

Where it is the children go.

JAMES STEPHENS

I Went Fishing

I went fishing,
Took some bait.
Didn't go early,
Didn't go late.

Caught eight fishes
To put in my pail.
Seven were mackerel,
But the eighth was a whale.

The seven were easy
To put into the tin,
But that whale caused me trouble
Before I packed him in!

Took my catch home.
What did Mother say?
"Get those eight fish out of here—
We're having steak today!"

UNKNOWN

The King's High Drummer

He was Bang bang banging on his
Big Bass Drum,
And the Regiment went marching to his
Thr-r-um, thrum thrum.
They came marching up the garden with their
Firm, hard tread,
A line of British soldiers with a Drummer
At their head.
They came March march marching through the
Wide front door,
And they clambered up the staircase to the
Second floor.

But, "It's tea-time, tea-time, come and
Wash your hands,"
Ordered Mummy to the leader of the
Regimental Bands:
She could hear him banging on his
Big Bass Drum,
But she didn't guess a Regiment was marching
To his Thr-r-um.
So the King's High Drummer put his

Drum away.
And he's going to play at Regiments
Another day:
He'll go Bang bang banging on his
Big Bass Drum.
And the corridor will echo to his
Thr-r-rum, thrum thrum.

CARYL BRAHMS

As I Was Coming Down the Stair

As I was coming down the stair
I met a man who wasn't there.
He wasn't there again today:
I *wish* that man would go away!

UNKNOWN

Toucannery

whatever one toucan can do
is sooner done by toucans two
and three toucans it's very true
can do much more than two can do

and toucans numbering two plus two can
manage more than all the zoo can
in fact there is no toucan who can
do what four or three or two can.

JACK PRELUTSKY

King's Cross

King's Cross.
What shall we do?
His purple robe
Is rent in two!
Out of his crown
He's torn the gems!
He's thrown his sceptre
Into the Thames!
The Court is shaking
In its shoe.
King's Cross
What shall we do?
Leave him alone for a minute or two.

ELEANOR FARJEON

The Song of the Engine

(slowly)

With snort and pant the engine dragged
    Its heavy train uphill,
And puffed these words the while she puffed
    And laboured with a will:

(Very slowly)

"I think—I can—I think—I can,
    I've got—to reach—the top,
I'm sure—I can—I will—get there,
    I sim—ply must—not stop!"

(More quickly)

At last the top was reached and passed,
    And then—how changed the song!
The wheels all joined in the engine's joy,
    As quickly she tore along!

(Very fast)

"I knew I could do it, I knew I could win,
    Oh, rickety rackety rack!
And now for a roaring rushing race
    On my smooth and shining track!"

H. WORSLEY-BENISON

46

A Baby Sardine

A baby Sardine
Saw her first submarine:
She was scared and watched through a peephole.

"Oh, come, come, come,"
Said the Sardine's mum,
"It's only a tin full of people."

SPIKE MILLIGAN

The Tadpole

Underneath the water-weeds
    Small and black, I wriggle,
And life is most surprising!
    Wiggle! waggle! wiggle!
There's every now and then a most
    Exciting change in me,
I wonder, wiggle! waggle!
    What I *shall* turn out to be!

E. E. GOULD

High June

Fiddle-de-dee!
Grasshoppers three,
Rollicking over the meadow;
Scarcely the grass,
Bends as they pass,
So fairy-light is their tread, O!

Said Grasshopper One,
"The summer's begun,
This sunshine is driving me crazy!"
Said Grasshopper Two,
"I feel just like you!"
And leapt to the top of a daisy.

"Please wait for me!"
Cried Grasshopper Three,
"My legs are ready for hopping!"
So grasshoppers three,
Fiddle-de-dee,
Raced all the day without stopping.

CATHERINE A. MORIN

48

The Black Pebble

There went three children down to the shore,
Down to the shore and back;
There was skipping Susan and bright-eyed Sam
And little scowling Jack.

Susan found a white cockle-shell,
The prettiest ever seen,
And Sam picked up a piece of glass,
Rounded and smooth and green.

But Jack found only a plain black pebble
That lay by the rolling sea,
And that was all that ever he found;
So back they went all three.

The cockle-shell they put on the table,
The green glass on the shelf,
But the little black pebble that Jack had found,
He kept it for himself.

JAMES REEVES

The Dragon with a Big Nose

The dragon
with a big nose
and twelve toes
on each foot
eats flies
and mince pies

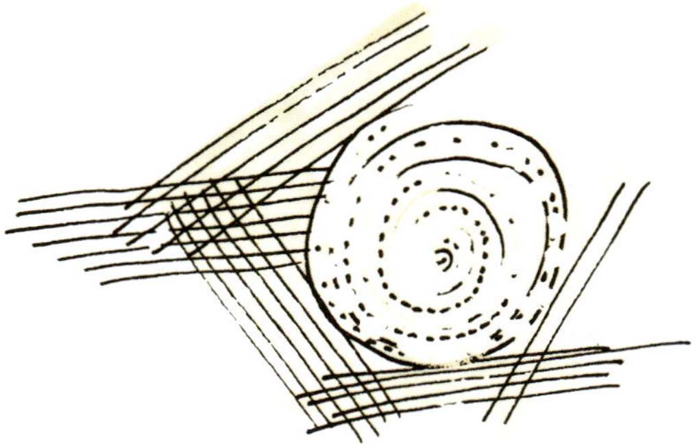

and sometimes
when he's very bad
whole towns
upside down

streets and houses
shops and churches
schools and fact'ries
undergrounds

swallows them all
quite whole
and spits out the glass fast
treading very carefully
somewhere else
going away.

No one's ever seen him coming;
they can't see him leave.
No one's ever seen him anyway
. . . . except me!

KATHY HENDERSON

Noise

I like noise.
The huffing,
the puffing
and buffing of a train.

The teaming,
and splashing,
and streaming of the rain.

The clashing
and bashing
and smashing of the plates.

The making
the baking
and scoffing of the cakes.

CHILD AUTHOR, UNKNOWN

A-Apple Pie

Little Pollie Pillikins
Peeped into the kitchen,
"H'm," says she, "Ho!" says she,
"Nobody there!"
Only little meeny mice,
Miniken and miching
On the broad flagstones, empty and bare.

Greedy Pollie Pillikins
Crept into the pantry.
There stood an Apple Pasty
Sugar white as snow.
Off the shelf she toppled it,
Quick and quiet and canty,
And the meeny mice they watched her
On her tip-tap-toe.
"Thief, Pollie Pillikins!"
Crouching in the shadows there,
Flickering in the candle-shining,
Fee, fo, fum!
Munching up the pastry,
Crunching up the apples,

53

"Thief!" squeaked the smallest mouse,
"Pollie, spare a crumb."

WALTER DE LA MARE

Horrible Things

"What's the horriblest thing you've seen?"
Said Nell to Jean.
"Some grey-coloured, trodden-on plasticine;
On a plate, a left-over cold baked bean;
A cloak-room ticket numbered thirteen;
A slice of meat without any lean;
The smile of a spiteful fairy-tale queen;
A thing in the sea like a brown submarine;
A cheese fur-coated in brilliant green;
A bluebottle perched on a piece of sardine.
What's the horriblest thing *you've* seen?"
Said Jean to Nell.

"Your face, as you tell
Of all the horriblest things you've seen."

ROY FULLER

The Night Wind

There's someone tapping at the window,
There's someone whispering at the door,
There's someone creeping through below there
And lifting up the carpet from the floor.

Shush! There's a crying and a moaning.
Hist! What a racket and a din!
Ho! Such a roaring in the chimney.
'Tis the night wind trying to get in.

CATHERINE A. MORIN

Good King Wenceslas

Good King Wenceslas looked out
On a cabbage garden:
He bumped into a Brussels sprout
And said, "I beg your pardon."

ENGLISH CHILDREN'S STREET RHYME

Hipporhinostricow

Such a beast is the Hipporhinostricow,
How it got so mixed up we'll never know how;
It sleeps all day and whistles all night,
And it wears yellow socks which are far too tight.

If you laugh at the Hipporhinostricow,
You're bound to get into an awful row;
The creature is protected, you see,
From silly people like you and me.

SPIKE MILLIGAN

Quack

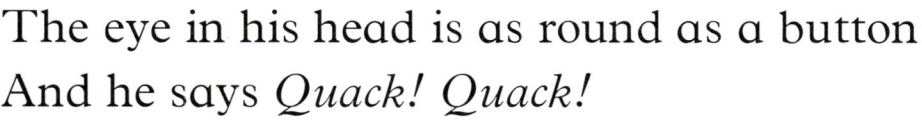

The duck is whiter than whey is,
His tail tips up over his back.
The eye in his head is as round as a button
And he says *Quack! Quack!*

He swims on his bright blue mill-pond,
By the willow-tree under the shack,
Then stands on his head to see down to the bottom,
And says, *Quack! Quack!*

When Molly steps out of the kitchen,
For apron—pinned round with a sack—
He squints at her round face,
   her dish and what's in it,
And says, *Quack! Quack!*

He preens the pure snow of his feathers
In the sun by the wheat-straw stack;
At dusk waddles home with his brothers and sisters
And says, *Quack! Quack!*

WALTER DE LA MARE

Snail

"I'm sorry I can't put you up"—
The snail said to her friend,
"For tho' the house is all my own
And—as you know—I live alone,
One room is all there is inside
And that, of course,
                          is
                                occupied!"

JOHN TOMPKINS

The Dodo

The Dodo used to walk around
And take the sun and air,
The Sun yet warms his native ground—
The Dodo is not there!
That voice which used to squawk and squeak
Is now forever dumb—
Yet you see his bones and beak
All in the Museum.

HILAIRE BELLOC

Winter Morning

Winter is the king of showmen,
Turning tree stumps into snow men
And houses into birthday cakes
And spreading sugar over lakes.
Smooth and clean and frosty white,
The world looks good enough to bite.
That's the season to be young,
Catching snowflakes on your tongue.

Snow is snowy when it's snowing,
I'm sorry it's slushy when it's going.

OGDEN NASH

59

There Was an Old Woman

There was an old woman who swallowed a fly;
I wonder why
She swallowed a fly.
Poor old woman, she's sure to die.

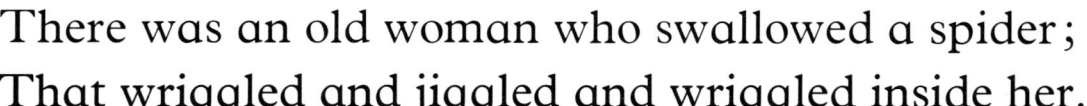

There was an old woman who swallowed a spider;
That wriggled and jiggled and wriggled inside her.
She swallowed the spider to catch the fly.
I wonder why
She swallowed the fly.
Poor old woman, she's sure to die.

There was an old woman who swallowed a bird;
How absurd
To swallow a bird.
She swallowed the bird to catch the spider
That wriggled and jiggled and wriggled inside her.
She swallowed the spider to catch the fly.
I wonder why
She swallowed the fly.
Poor old woman, she's sure to die.

There was an old woman who swallowed a cat;
Fancy that!
She swallowed a cat.
She swallowed the cat to catch the bird,
She swallowed the bird to catch the spider
That wriggled and jiggled and wriggled inside her.
She swallowed the spider to catch the fly.
I wonder why
She swallowed the fly.
Poor old woman, she's sure to die.

There was an old woman who swallowed a dog;
She went the whole hog
And swallowed a dog.
She swallowed the dog to catch the cat,
She swallowed the cat to catch the bird,
She swallowed the bird to catch the spider
That wriggled and jiggled and wriggled inside her.
She swallowed the spider to catch the fly.
I wonder why
She swallowed the fly.
Poor old woman, she's sure to die.

There was an old woman who swallowed a cow;
I wonder how
She swallowed a cow.
She swallowed a cow to catch the dog,
She swallowed the dog to catch the cat,
She swallowed the cat to catch the bird,
She swallowed the bird to catch the spider
That wriggled and jiggled and wriggled inside her.
She swallowed the spider to catch the fly.
I wonder why
She swallowed a fly.
Poor old woman, she's sure to die.

There was an old woman who swallowed a horse.
She died, of course!

TRADITIONAL

Song for a Ball-game

Bounce ball! Bounce ball!
    One—two—three.
Underneath my right leg
    And round about my knee.
Bounce ball! Bounce ball!
    Bird—or—bee
Flying from the rose-bud
    Up into the tree.

Bounce ball! Bounce ball!
    Fast—you—go
Underneath my left leg
    And round about my toe.
Bounce ball! Bounce ball!
    Butt—er—fly
Flying from the rosebud
    Up into the sky.

Bounce ball! Bounce ball!
    You—can't—stop.
Right leg and left leg
    Round them both you hop.
Bounce ball! Bounce ball!
    Shy—white—dove,
Tell me how to find him,
    My own true love.

WILFRED THORLEY

The Cats of Kilkenny

There were once two cats of Kilkenny,
Each thought there was one cat too many;
So they fought and they fit,
And they scratched and they bit,
Till, excepting their nails
And the tips of their tails,
Instead of two cats, there weren't any!

UNKNOWN

Seven and a Half

Contents

The Hen and the Carp

Once, in a roostery
There lived a speckled hen, and when—
Ever she laid an egg this hen
Ecstatically cried:
"O progeny miraculous, particular spectaculous,
What a wonderful hen am I!"

Down in a pond nearby
Perchance a fat and broody carp
Was basking, but her ears were sharp—
She heard Dame Cackle cry:
"O progeny miraculous, particular spectaculous,
What a wonderful hen am I!"

"Ah, Cackle," bubbled she,
For your single egg, O silly one,
I lay at least a million;
Suppose for each I cried:
"O progeny miraculous, particular spectaculous!
What a hullaballoo there'd be."

IAN SERRAILLIER

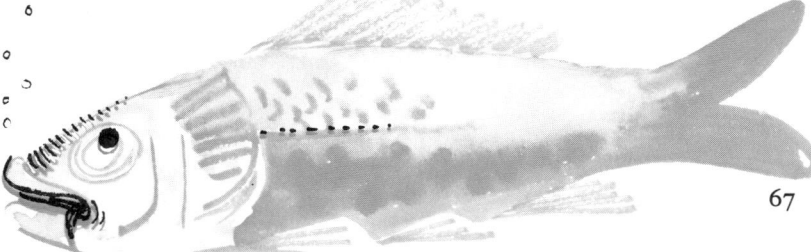

67

The Bongaloo

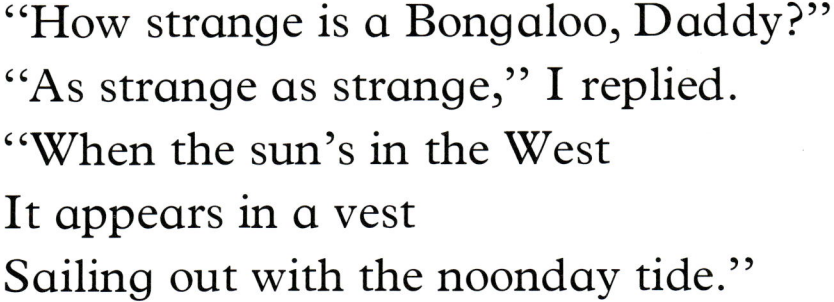

"What is a Bongaloo, Daddy?"
"A Bongaloo, Son," said I,
"Is a tall bag of cheese
Plus a Chinaman's knees
And the leg of a nanny goat's eye."

"How strange is a Bongaloo, Daddy?"
"As strange as strange," I replied.
"When the sun's in the West
It appears in a vest
Sailing out with the noonday tide."

"What shape is a Bongaloo, Daddy?"
"The shape, my Son, I'll explain:
It's tall round the nose
Which continually grows
In the general direction of Spain."

"Are you *sure* there's a Bongaloo, Daddy?"
"Am I sure, my Son?" said I.
"Why, I've seen it, not quite,
On a dark sunny night.
Do you think that I'd tell you a lie?"

SPIKE MILLIGAN

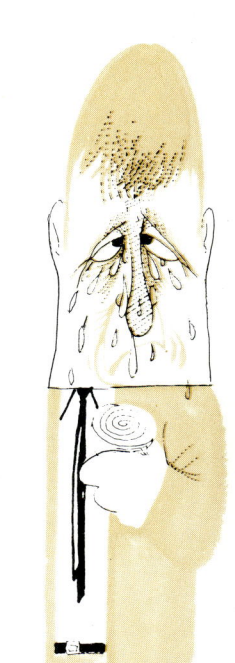

The Man in the Onion Bed

I met a man in an onion bed.
He was crying so hard his eyes were red.
And the tears ran off the end of his nose
As he ate his way down the onion rows.

He ate and he cried, but for all his tears
He sang, "Sweet onions, oh my dears!
I love you, I do, and you love me,
But you make me as sad as a man can be."

JOHN CIARDI

Drawing

Small boys and girls can draw a house
But find it hard to draw a mouse.

Most drawing in a house is square:
Square walls and windows in square air.

—Though from the chimneys, I don't doubt,
Nothing square can ever come out.

But smoke is really only scribble:
Not so the beast that loves to nibble.

You'd need a film to show a nose
That always quivers as it goes.

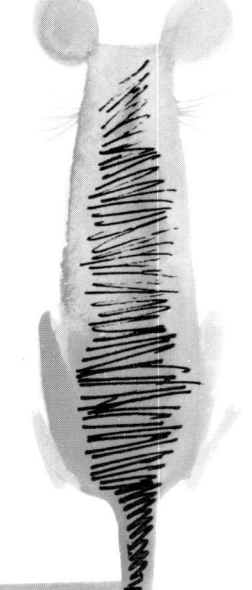

Even invisible ink wouldn't meet
The problem of tiny rapid feet.

If you were colouring the fur—
Grey or brown, which would you prefer?

And were you getting down the tail
And put a corner in, you'd fail.

And how to show those long front teeth,
The bottom lip tucked underneath:

The upper ditto very bristly?
Your style would have to be quite Whistlery.

Besides, a mouse would never keep still
Long enough to let you draw it well.

And were one brought in by the cat
You'd be too sad to copy that.

Strange that a mixture of curves and hair
Likes living in a thing so square:

It could, were it self-advertising,
Make life and art much more surprising.

ROY FULLER

71

The Snowflake

Before I melt
Come, look at me!
This lovely, icy filigree!
Of a great forest
In one night
I make a wilderness
Of white:
By skyey cold
Of crystals made,
All softly on
Your fingers laid,
I pause, that you
My beauty see:
Breathe, and I vanish
Instantly.

WALTER DE LA MARE

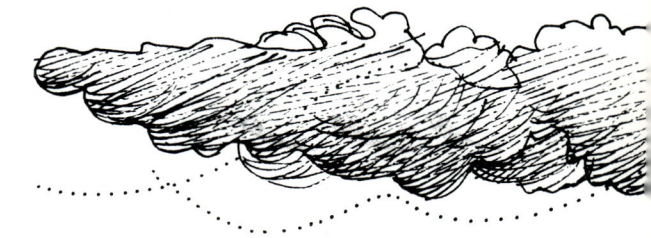

The Wind

I can get through the doorway without any key,
And strip the leaves from the great oak tree.

I can drive storm-clouds and shake tall towers,
Or steal through a garden and not wake flowers.

Seas I can move and ships I can sink;
I can carry a house-top or the scent of a pink.

When I am angry I can rave and riot,
And when I am spent, I lie quiet as quiet.

JAMES REEVES

Flo, the White Duck

All white and smooth is Flo
A-swimming:
Her lovely dress is plain—
No trimming.
A neat delight,
She fans to left and right
The silver-rippled pond.
Behind her, safe and fond,
Her yellow ducklings bob and skim,
Yellow, fluffy, trim.

But all a-waddle and a-spraddle goes Flo
A-walking;
A clacking voice she has
For talking.
In slimy ooze
She plants enormous shoes
And squelches, squat and slow.
Behind her in a row
Her ducklings dip and paddle
And try to spraddle.

GWEN DUNN

The Frog

Be kind and tender to the Frog,
    And do not call him names,
As "Slimy skin" or "Polly-wog",
    Or otherwise "Ugly James",
Or "Gap-a-grin", or "Toad-gone-wrong",
    or "Billy Bandy-knees".
The Frog is justly sensitive
    To epithets like these.
No animal will more repay
    A treatment kind and fair;
At least so lonely people say
Who keep a frog (and, by the way,
They are extremely rare).

HILAIRE BELLOC

Mother Knows Best

I've lots of pets, some small, some big—
a cat, a rabbit, a guinea-pig,
a budgie, dear to all of us
and Oliver, my octopus.
Oliver's a bit of a freak,
he has two eyes, a parrot beak,
a jelly-bag belly,
shaped like a gong
and eight rubber arms, each three feet long.
Mum says Oliver's dangerous.
Well, you know what Mums are. Ridiculous.
How can Oliver, gentle and dumb,
climb out of his aquarium?

Mystery of mysteries, one day
Belle the budgie flew away.
Two days later, just as weird,
Gilbert the guinea-pig disappeared.

I fed my pets next day—good habit—
but where was Reginald, my rabbit?
Caroline, my tortoise-shell cat
had gone the morning after that.

Mum cried, for Mum was fond of her,
when Oliver began to purr.
I went to bed at ten to nine,
sobbing for dear friends of mine—
Belle, Gilbert, Reginald, Caroline.
I'd nearly cried myself to sleep
when I heard something or someone creep
very quietly, on all four pairs
of plop, plop, plop, plop feet upstairs.
My hair and I stood up with fright.
My heart went mad.
Oh, was I glad
I'd locked my bedroom door that night.
Maybe, after all, Mum was right.

R. C. SCRIVEN

My Brother Bert

Pets are the Hobby of my brother Bert.
He used to go to school with a Mouse in his shirt.

His Hobby, it grew, as some hobbies will,
And it grew and GREW and GREW until

Oh, don't breathe a word, pretend you haven't heard.
A simply appalling thing has occurred—

The very thought makes me iller and iller;
Bert's brought home a gigantic Gorilla!

If you think that's really not such a scare,
What if it quarrels with his Grizzly Bear?

You still think you could keep your head?
What if the lion from under the bed

And the four ostriches that deposit
Their football eggs in his bedroom closet

And the Aardvark out of his bottom drawer
All danced out and joined in the Roar?

What if the Pangolins were to caper
Out of their nests behind the wall paper?

With the fifty sorts of Bats
That hang on his hat-stand like old hats,

And out of a shoebox the excitable Platypus
Along with the Ocelot or Jungle-Cattypus?

The Wombat, the Dingo, the Gecko, the Grumpus—
How they would shake the house with their Rumpus!

Not to forget the Bandycoot
Who would certainly peer from his battered old boot.

Why, it would be a dreadful day,
And what, Oh what would the neighbours say?

TED HUGHES

The Paint Box

"Cobalt and amber and ultramarine,
Ivory black and emerald green—
What shall I paint to give pleasure to you?"
"Paint for me somebody utterly new."

"I have painted you tigers in crimson and white."
"The colours were good and you painted aright."
"I have painted the cook and a camel in blue
And a panther in purple." "You painted them true."

"Now mix me a colour that nobody knows,
And paint me a country where nobody goes.
And put in it people a little like you,
Watching a unicorn drinking the dew."

E. V. RIEU

Miss T.

It's a very odd thing—
    As odd as can be—
That whatever Miss T. eats
    Turns into Miss T.;
Porridge and apples,
    Mince, muffins and mutton,
Jam, junket, jumbles—
    Not a rap, not a button
It matters; the moment
    They're out of her plate,
Though shared by Miss Butcher
    And sour Mr. Bate;
Tiny and cheerful,
    And neat as can be,
Whatever Miss T. eats
    Turns into Miss T.

WALTER DE LA MARE

81

The Hairy Dog

My dog's so furry I've not seen
His face for years and years:
His eyes are buried out of sight,
I only guess his ears.

When people ask me for his breed
I do not know or care:
He has the beauty of them all
Hidden beneath his hair.

HERBERT ASQUITH

The Centipede

A centipede was happy quite,
Until a frog in fun
Said, "Pray, which leg comes after which?"
This raised her mind to such a pitch,
She lay distracted in a ditch
Considering how to run.

MRS. EDMUND CRASTER

Daddy Fell into the Pond

Everyone grumbled. The sky was grey.
We had nothing to do and nothing to say.
We were nearing the end of a dismal day,
And there seemed to be nothing beyond,
       THEN
Daddy fell into the pond!

And everyone's face grew merry and bright,
And Timothy danced for sheer delight.
"Give me a camera, quick, oh quick!
He's crawling out of the duckweed. Click!"

Then the gardener suddenly slapped his knee,
And doubled up, shaking silently,
And the ducks all quacked as if they were daft
And it sounded as if the old drake laughed.

O, there wasn't a thing that didn't respond
       WHEN
Daddy fell into the pond!

ALFRED NOYES

The Spinning Earth

The earth, they say,
spins round and round.
It doesn't look it
from the ground,
and never makes
a spinning sound.

And water never
swirls and swishes
from oceans full
of dizzy fishes,
and shelves don't lose
their pans and dishes.

And houses don't go whirling by,
or puppies swirl around the sky,
or robins spin instead of fly.

It may be true
what people say
about one spinning
night and day . . .
but I keep wondering, anyway.

AILEEN FISHER

A Mermaid Song

She sits by the sea in the clear, shining air,
And the sailors call her Moonlight, Moonlight;
They see her smoothing her wavy hair
And they hear her singing, singing.
The sea shells learn their tunes from her
And the big fish listen with never a stir
To catch the voice of Moonlight, Moonlight,
And I would hark for a year and a year
To hear her singing, singing.

JAMES REEVES

A Rainy Day

The sky is grey today,
The birds swoop low.
Trees are black as night,
A robin hops along the wet wall top,
His breast is the brightest thing on this dull day.
Water drips from the trees,
Raindrops are like jewels on the grass,
The path shines like a stream,
But soon the clouds will float away.
The sun will shine more brightly after rain,
The birds will flap their wings for joy,
The jewels will dissolve in the grass,
And I will ride my bike again.

A POEM BY ANDREW WEST, AGED SEVEN

Sing a Song of People

Sing a song of people
    Walking fast or slow;
People in the city,
    Up and down they go.

People on the sidewalk,
People on the bus;
People passing, passing,
In back and front of us.
People on the subway
Underneath the ground;
People riding taxis
Round and round and round.

People with their hats on,
Going in the doors;
People with umbrellas
When it rains and pours.
People in tall buildings

87

And in stores below;
Riding elevators
Up and down they go.

People walking singly,
People in a crowd;
People saying nothing,
People talking loud.
People laughing, smiling,
Grumpy people too;
People who just hurry
And never look at you!

Sing a song of people
    Who like to come and go;
Sing of city people
    You see but never know!

LOIS LENSKI

Good Night, Mouser!

"Good Night, Mouser!"

The front door closes,
The bolt slides home,
And Mouser hops down into the garden,
A cat unwanted, alone.

The late-night neighbour,
Hurrying along
Click-clack on the empty street,
Feels a sudden fur at his feet.
Wondering he bends,
And Mouser winds about him,
Furring him,
Purring him,
Most pleadingly.
For even in the dark, Mouser knows his friends.
But the neighbour rises and feels for his key:
"Good night, Mouser!
Run away now and play!"
And Mouser wanders away.

All the long night he'll stray
Through empty garden, or waste and thorny patch,
Nosing at a pebble or a snail
In the flower-bed;
His ears straining to catch
The squeak of a fallen fledgling, not yet dead:
His paws ready to snatch
At the scuttering rat,
Or the beaded mouse with the flickering tail.
All the long night, prowling and prying
Around the cold roots of the thorns;
Or sometimes just lying
In a tuft of grass,
Just lying in wait, no more.

But when daylight dawns
He is back at the door—
Back with his doorstep offering of rat or mouse;
And he sits with uplifted chin,
Endlessly patient, watching the house,
Watching for the twitch of the curtain,
Waiting for the slide of the bolt,
And the voice that cries, "Come in!"

Stay in tonight, Mouser!
Quick, up the stairs before others can see!
No longer alone,
NOT a cat-without-a-home,
Stay warm in my bed with me!

JOHN WALSH

The Little Crocodile

How doth the little crocodile
Improve his shining tail,
And pour the waters of the Nile
On every golden scale!

How cheerfully he seems to grin,
How neatly spreads his claws,
And welcomes little fishes in
With gently smiling jaws!

LEWIS CARROLL

There Was a Naughty Boy

There was a naughty boy,
And a naughty boy was he.
He ran away to Scotland
The people for to see.
Then he found
    That the ground
    Was as hard,
    That a yard
    Was as long,
    That a song
    Was as merry,
    That a cherry
    Was as red,
    That lead
    Was as weighty,
    That fourscore
    Was as eighty,
    That a door
    Was as wooden
    As in England.

So he stood in his shoes
And he wondered,
He wondered.
He stood in his shoes
And he wondered.

JOHN KEATS

Windy Nights

Whenever the moon and stars are set,
    Whenever the wind is high,
All night long in the dark and wet,
    A man goes riding by.
Late in the night when the fires are out,
Why does he gallop and gallop about?

Whenever the trees are crying aloud,
    And ships are tossed at sea,
By, on the highway, low and loud,
    By at the gallop goes he:
By at the gallop he goes, and then
By he comes back at the gallop again.

ROBERT LOUIS STEVENSON

Dan the Watchman

Dan the Watchman
Doesn't go to bed.
He sits in a little wooden hut
Instead;
At a little coke-fire,
Half red, half blue,
Listening to the owls
Go "Whoo! Whoo! Whoo!"
And the Town Hall clock
Strike half-past two.

When the moon sits on top
Of the grey church spire,
He puts more coke
On his red-and-blue fire;
When the old mill pond
Begins to freeze,
He eats his supper
Of bread and cheese.

I'd like to go out
In the middle of the night,
When the little coke fire
Is shining bright,
When the flames turn blue
And the flames burn red,
And everyone else in the world is in bed.
Then I'd sit in the little wooden hut with Dan
And drink strong tea from his black billy can.

JOHN D. SHERIDAN

Tongue Twisters

Weather

Whether the weather be fine
Or whether the weather be not,
Whether the weather be cold
Or whether the weather be hot,
We'll weather the weather
Whatever the weather,
Whether we like it or not.

UNKNOWN

A Woodchuck

How much wood would a woodchuck chuck
If a woodchuck would chuck wood?
It would chuck what wood a woodchuck would
    chuck
If a woodchuck would chuck wood.

UNKNOWN